The Bones of Fred McFee

Eve Bunting

ILLUSTRATED BY Kurt Cyrus

VOYAGER BOOKS
HARCOURT, INC.

Orlando   Austin   New York   San Diego   Toronto   London

For information about permission to reproduce selections from this book,
write to trade.permissions@hmhco.com or to Permissions, Houghton Mifflin
Harcourt Publishing Company, 3 Park Avenue, 19th Floor, New York, New York 10016.

www.hmhco.com

First Voyager Books edition 2005
Voyager Books is a trademark of Harcourt, Inc., registered in the
United States of America and/or other jurisdictions.

The Library of Congress has cataloged the hardcover edition as follows:
Bunting, Eve, 1928–
The bones of Fred McFee/Eve Bunting; illustrated by Kurt Cyrus.
p.   cm.
Summary: A toy skeleton at Halloween provides menace and mystery.
[1. Halloween—Fiction.   2. Stories in rhyme.]   I. Cyrus, Kurt, ill.   II. Title.
PZ8.3.B92Bo   2002
[E]—dc21   2001002414
ISBN 0-15-202004-7
ISBN 0-15-205423-5 pb

SCP   15 14 13 12 11 10
4500659527

The illustrations in this book were done in scratchboard and watercolor.
The display lettering was created by Judythe Sieck.
The text type was set in Raleigh.
Color separations by Bright Arts Ltd., Hong Kong
Printed and bound by RR Donnelley,China
Production supervision by Pascha Gerlinger
Designed by Judythe Sieck

For all the ghosts I've never met
—E. B.

For pumpkin heads everywhere
—K. C.

There's a skeleton high in our sycamore tree,
High as high can be.
He was hung up there by my sister and me,
High in our sycamore tree.

His bones are white and he's long and lean,
There in our sycamore tree.
His teeth are the biggest we've ever seen,
Grinning at Jessie and me.

We brought him home from the harvest fair
And named him Fred McFee.
He looks so scary dangling there,
High in our sycamore tree.

He isn't real, but it's hard to tell—
He's plastic, head to toe.
But all of his bones are joined so well,
No one would ever know!

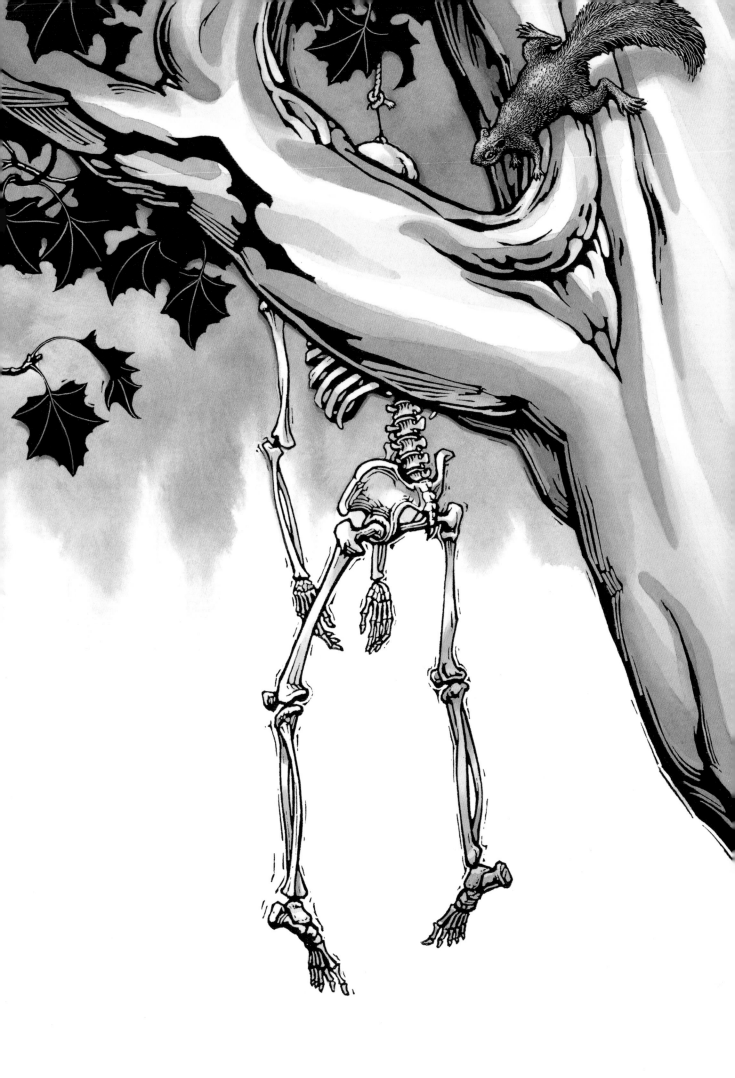

At night when the wind howls overhead,
With ghoulish, ghastly glee,
Our skeleton dances the dance of the dead,
There in our sycamore tree.

We'd like to take a peek out back,
But who knows what we'd see!
We hear those bones go *clickety-clack*,
The bones of Fred McFee.

Our old dog, Sam, once snapped at flies,
Around our sycamore tree.
Now Sam stays home and the flies don't rise—
It's such a mystery!

Our rooster used to crow all day,
Up in our sycamore tree.
Now the rooster's gone and the hens won't lay,
Since we got Fred McFee.

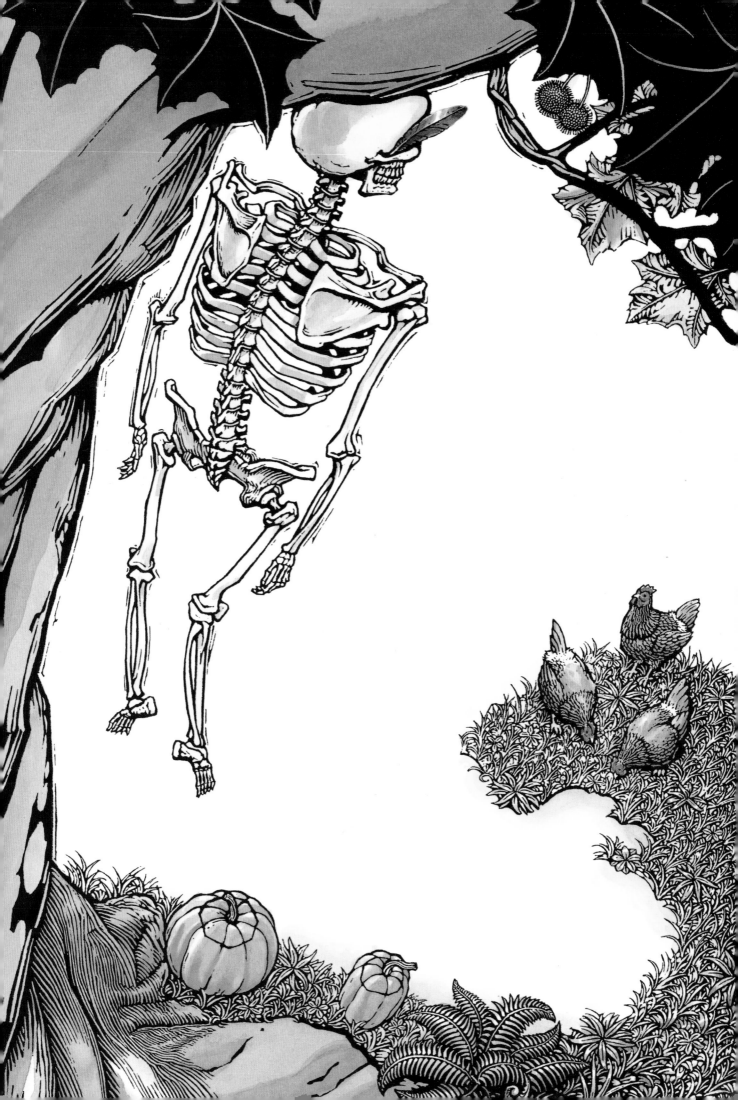

A great horned owl with yellow eyes
Sits in our sycamore tree.
When we look up, those gleaming eyes
Are all that we can see.

We'll let Fred hang till Halloween—
He won't come down before.
We'll hide him where he can't be seen,
Till Halloween comes once more.

The dark is dropping like a cowl—
There's no star to be seen.

What's wrong with Sam? We hear him howl,
This night of Halloween.

The morning's bright and filled with light.
But where is Fred McFee?
His bones have vanished in the night,
Gone from our sycamore tree.

Did someone come by dead of night,
With only the owl to see?
Did someone come by pale moonlight
And cut down Fred McFee?

There's a mound below that's long and lean,
Beneath our sycamore tree.
And the mound is brown, not frosty green. . . .
We know what it might be.

We know it's a grave out there on the slope,
Beneath our sycamore tree.
But who could it be that cut the rope
That held up Fred McFee?

The grave sinks low and we mark the spot
With pebbles and shells from the sea.
We hope that Fred will like it a lot
And sleep contentedly.

But . . .

When the wind howls overhead
And shakes our sycamore tree,
We hear them dancing the dance of the dead—

The bones of Fred McFee!